FALKIRK

D1079237

This Diary
Belongs To

Pip!

To my niece, Natalie,
with fairy best wishes – A. D.
For Millie – V. C.

First published 2008 by
Walker Books Ltd
87 Vauxhall Walk
London SE11 5HJ

This edition published 2012

2 4 6 8 10 9 7 5 3 1

Text © 2008 Alan Durant
Illustrations © 2008 Vanessa Cabban

The right of Alan Durant and Vanessa Cabban to be identified as
author and illustrator respectively of this work has been asserted by them
in accordance with the Copyright, Designs and Patents Act 1988

This book has been typeset in Centaur MT Regular

Printed and bound in Great Britain by Clays Ltd, St Ives plc

All rights reserved. No part of this book may be reproduced,
transmitted or stored in an information retrieval system
in any form or by any means, graphic, electronic or mechanical,
including photocopying, taping and recording,
without prior written permission from the publisher.

British Library Cataloguing in Publication Data:
a catalogue record for this book is available
from the British Library

ISBN 978-1-4063-4043-3

www.walker.co.uk

Diary of a Tooth Fairy

EAST AYRSHIRE LIBRARIES	
484563	
Bertrams	19/07/2012
	£4.99

ALAN DURANT

ILLUSTRATED BY

VANESSA CABBAN

WALKER BOOKS

AND SUBSIDIARIES

LONDON · BOSTON · SYDNEY · AUCKLAND

The Tooth Fairy
Training School

The Tooth, The Whole Tooth
And Nothing But The Tooth

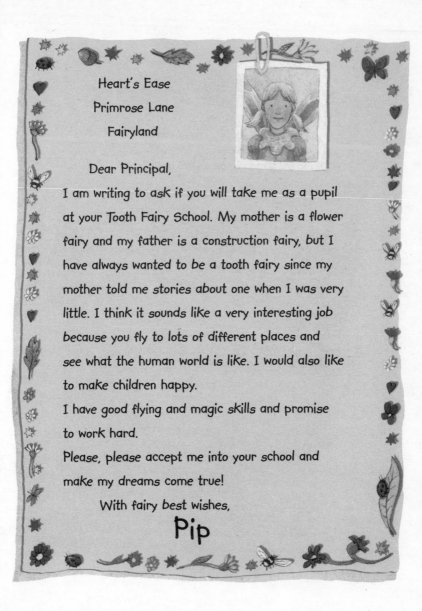

Heart's Ease
Primrose Lane
Fairyland

Dear Principal,

I am writing to ask if you will take me as a pupil
at your Tooth Fairy School. My mother is a flower
fairy and my father is a construction fairy, but I
have always wanted to be a tooth fairy since my
mother told me stories about one when I was very
little. I think it sounds like a very interesting job
because you fly to lots of different places and
see what the human world is like. I would also like
to make children happy.

I have good flying and magic skills and promise
to work hard.

Please, please accept me into your school and
make my dreams come true!

With fairy best wishes,

Pip

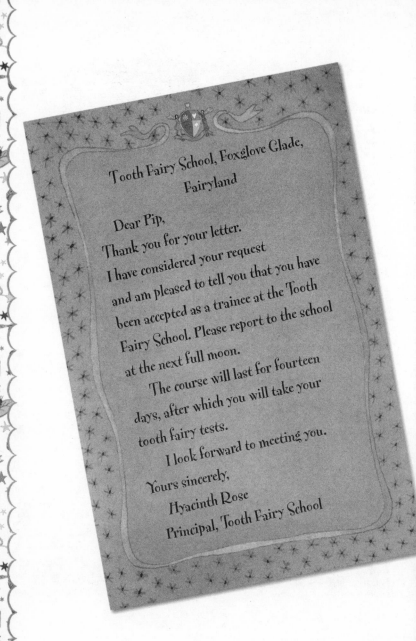

Tooth Fairy School, Foxglove Glade,
Fairyland

Dear Pip,

Thank you for your letter.
I have considered your request
and am pleased to tell you that you have
been accepted as a trainee at the Tooth
Fairy School. Please report to the school
at the next full moon.

The course will last for fourteen
days, after which you will take your
tooth fairy tests.

I look forward to meeting you.

Yours sincerely,

Hyacinth Rose
Principal, Tooth Fairy School

Day One

Here I am at the school for trainee tooth fairies. Me, Pip! I am sooo excited. No one in my family has ever trained to be a tooth fairy before. My mum says she is very proud of me – and I haven't even started the course yet! For the next couple of weeks this

school will be my home – I hope
I don't get homesick.

Today was settling in and
introductions day. First we
gathered in the hall to meet the
principal, Hyacinth Rose.

She is a very
important fairy.
She has silver wing
tips, which are the sign
of the highest rank of tooth fairy.
She has trained most of the tooth

fairies working today and is on first name terms with the Fairy Queen! She is quite old and stern-looking and does not seem to smile very much.

Hyacinth Rose warned us that being a tooth fairy is a very big responsibility, not a game, and that the training would be tough.

"If you don't like hard work then you should leave right away," she said, and she gave us all a long hard stare – but no one left.

"Well, that's a good start," she said.

At the end of the meeting Hyacinth Rose handed us our timetable for the first week of training. Now I see what she means about hard work!

After the meeting she took us to our dorm. It is quite bare, but each of us has our own hammock to sleep in. I tried mine out straight away. It's really comfy and great for bouncing about in. I bounced so hard that I fell out! Luckily I wasn't hurt, but Hyacinth Rose wasn't impressed.

"Pip, isn't it?" she said.

"Yes," I replied very quietly, blushing.

"I know your mother, May," she said. "And I imagine she is very proud that you are at this school."

"Yes," I said.

"Well then, Pip, I suggest that you try a little harder to make yourself worthy of that pride." She gave me that long hard stare that could probably wither a flower if she wanted it to.

"Yes, ma'am," I muttered. "I won't do it again."

"See that you don't," said Hyacinth Rose, then off she went. Not the best

start to my career as a tooth fairy!
I was feeling a bit down, but the
other trainees were very nice and
they made me feel better.

There are three of them.

Their names are Peasbody, Mab
and Niamh (that's how you write
it, but it sounds like Neeve).

We must be up
very early in the
morning for our
first proper day
of training, so
I'd better get
some sleep. Let's
hope I make a
better impression
tomorrow!

Day Two

Tinkle, tinkle CLANG!

We were woken at dawn by a bluebell chorus. It was Hyacinth Rose giving us our alarm call. The noise was so loud, I nearly fell out of my bed again!

"Time to get up," shouted HR

(that's what we trainees have
started to call her now – though
not to her face, of course!).
I didn't feel much like shining,
more like drizzling.

"Come along, Pip," HR
instructed. "This is no time to be
lying in bed. There's work
to be done."

"Yes ma'am,"
I yawned.

I had a delicious
breakfast of hazelnut
crunch and honey
washed down with fresh
dew and then I felt much better.

After breakfast HR introduced

us to Madame le Fey, who is
Professor of Dentricals at the
school. (I have no idea what that
means, but it is something to do
with teeth and sounds very
important!) She took
us for our first lesson.

"Now," she said. "Let us begin at ze beginning…" She waved her wand and a picture appeared on the board behind her.

"Voila! Ze tooth."

Peasbody sniggered. Madame le Fey was not amused. She said that teeth were not a laughing matter, they were the whole purpose of a tooth fairy's life. She pointed at the tooth with her wand. I thought she was over doing it a little. It was quite a nice tooth, but not that special.

The Professor set us a little test. She handed us all a picture showing different kinds of teeth.

Only one could be collected by a
tooth fairy, she said, and we had
to find it. She timed us with a
dandelion clock.

I looked at the different teeth
and ticked the one I thought was
correct. I hoped I was right...
And luckily, I was! Peasbody and

Niamh got the right answer too, but poor Mab got it wrong. She'd put a tick next to the set of false teeth.

"Ooh la-la," Madame le Fey tutted. "If you take zese, how will granny chew her food?"

She made us write all the names of the other teeth on the paper so that we would be able to identify them. Then she gave us another diagram showing the different kinds of human teeth.

A

?

B

WHICH TOOTH
SHOULD YOU
TAKE?

C

D

Later, in the dorm,
Mab was a bit upset about
getting her first test wrong so I
tried to cheer her up by turning
my diagram sheet into a paper
dart and throwing it across the
room. It flew beautifully and we
all cheered.

Unfortunately, at that moment,
HR walked in. The dart landed
right at her feet. She didn't say a

word. She just gave us that
withering look.

"To whom does this belong?"
she asked.

I said it was mine.

"Ah, Pip. I might have guessed,"
she sighed.

"Please, ma'am, she was giving us a demonstration on flight," said Niamh. "It was most interesting."

"Mmm, was it indeed?" HR muttered, as if she didn't believe a word. "Well, tomorrow you shall be doing some flying of your own. We shall be visiting the tooth fairy workshop for some practical lessons."

At last we're going to do something! I can't wait!

Roll on tomorrow.

Day Three

What a busy day! I am quite exhausted.

"Some people think that all there is to being a tooth fairy is flying around collecting children's teeth and looking gorgeous," said Hyacinth Rose when we arrived

at the tooth fairy workshop.

None of us said anything, because that's exactly what we all thought! How wrong we were…

I've never seen a place as busy as the tooth fairy workshop. There are fairies flying in with new teeth all the time. First they take them to the depository where all new teeth are logged in and sent for inspection.

After this, more fairies sort the teeth into piles of good and bad. Bad or broken teeth are passed to another group of fairies whose job is to mend them, then the mended teeth join the good teeth for polishing with beeswax and buffing with dandelion seed puffs.

We had to have a go at all the jobs.

The hardest one was carrying teeth from one place to the next. They weigh more than you think! My wings were quite flapped out by the end of it. My favourite bit was polishing and buffing. It was such fun! I worked really hard.

"Why, Pip, I do believe I can see my face in that tooth," said HR

when I'd finished. I was beaming
all over, as if I'd been polished and
buffed myself!

Peasbody and Niamh did very
well too – but poor Mab had another
disaster. She buffed her tooth so
hard that she broke the top off.
She started to cry. HR told her not
to be so silly – the tooth fairies would
fix the tooth in no time! She also said

that humans are always breaking
their teeth and that they take them
to a person called a dentist to be
mended.

I wonder what dentists look like.
Like this perhaps?

I can't write any more.
My hand is aching from all that
buffing!

Day Four

HR let us have a rest day today because we worked so hard yesterday. She said we'd better make the most of it because it will be the last one we get! We played games and asked each other riddles and got to know each other better. We had some really good wheat stalk fights,

but best of all was a game that
Peasbody showed us. It's called
Catch Petal. You fill a hazelnut
cup with daisy petals, then you throw
the petals in the air and see how
many you can catch on your wings.
Peasbody's ma says it's very good for
wing control. We all thought
it was lots of fun too.

   I think it's time
that I described
my fellow trainees.
First Peasbody.
She has dark skin with
long dark brown curly hair.

She loves to laugh and play tricks.
This morning she stood outside
the dorm door and pretended to
be HR.

"The last one up gets no breakfast,"
she barked and she sounded just like
HR, she really did.

Well, the rest of us tumbled out
of our beds so fast we ended up in
a big messy heap on the floor. Then
in came Peasbody giggling like a
pixie.

"Fooled you," she laughed.
And she had!

Mab is much quieter than Peasbody.

She's quite
shy in fact
and her
cheeks often
blush pink when she
does anything wrong.
I think she is a bit
homesick, so I try to talk
to her as much as I can
to make her feel more at
home. She has found the
course quite hard so far.

I like Peasbody and Mab, but I like Niamh best of all. She is very kind and friendly and since she stood up for me the other night we have been firm friends.

She comes from the Emerald Isle and tells the most brilliant stories. She says that when she was a baby her father took her to kiss the Blarney Stone (that's some famous stone where she lives) and it gave her the gift of storytelling. Today Niamh told us a tale about leprechauns.

"Is it true that there's a crock of gold at the end of the rainbow?" I asked her.

"To be sure it is," she replied.

"Then why hasn't anyone ever found the gold and taken it?" Mab enquired.

"Ah, because the gold is not real gold, it's the colour of your deepest wish and desire," said Niamh, "and nobody's is exactly the same."

Well, I know what my deepest wish and desire is: to be a tooth fairy!

Day Five

Another day with Madame le Fey and her Dentricals. She started with a question that really made us think: why do tooth fairies collect teeth? It was such an obvious question but we'd never thought about it before.

We'd seen teeth being brought to
the workshop and mended and
buffed up, but what happened to
them then? For a few moments we
all sat in silence feeling like fools —
and then it came to me.

"Please, ma'am," I said at last, "are they used for building things?"

Madame le Fey clapped her hands together and beamed. "Well done, Pip!" she cried.

"But what sort of things?"

Peasbody flapped her wings
excitedly.

"Walls," she said.

"Palaces," said Niamh.

"Chairs," said Mab.

"Fountains,"
I said.

Suddenly we were
full of answers.

"Baths."

"Boats."

"Beds."

"Lights."

"Tables."

"Cupboards."

"Statues."

Then Mab said, "Toilets",
and the rest of us burst out laughing.

Poor Mab went very pink. Madame le Fey frowned and sighed, but then she said, "Ah, well, ma fille, at least you are using your brain."

Then she gave us a sheet with pictures of tooth constructions and we had to draw one of our own. I drew a fairy cottage for my family to live in.

My mum would love it, I know!

Madame le Fey said that many magnificent fairy buildings have been made from human teeth. Tomorrow we are going to fly out to see some.

Later, when we got back to our dorm, we found a basket full of delicious fairy cakes that the school's cook, Basil, had baked for us. The basket was made out of a tooth of course, but luckily the cakes weren't! They were made of saffron and lovely honey – fresh from the bee.

Day Six

Poor Peasbody wasn't
feeling well today.
Her face was green
as a leprechaun's.
I think she might
have eaten too

46

many cakes last night!

So while Peasbody stayed in bed,
the rest of us flew off around
Fairyland for the day.

Basil made us a delicious packed
lunch of mallow fruits, fairy bread

and nettle juice — and left over cakes,
of course!

Hyacinth Rose gave us each a
different map with five sites — or
"wonders" as she called them —
marked on it. We each had to fly off

and find them, then describe them
to the others when we got back. I
decided to draw pictures of mine so
I'd remember what they looked like.

My five wonders
of the
fairy world

"Map reading is very important
for tooth fairies," said HR. "You
cannot always rely on your fairy
magic to find places. Let's see how
you get on."

She asked us if we had any questions, and Mab asked which way up the map went. HR gave her one of those withering looks and said she should be able to work that out for herself. Poor Mab went as red as a rosehip.

Each of us flew off in a different direction. I went south. Well, no, I was supposed to go south. I actually started going north, until I realized I had the map upside down – Mab's question wasn't so silly after all!

I got lost a few times, but eventually I reached my first site: Tooth Tower.

It was amazing! It was so tall it almost touched the clouds. I flew up to the top and had the most fantastic view of Fairyland. I thought I could see the school far away in the distance. I wondered if Peasbody was still in her hammock.

The second site was magnificent! It was a stunning statue of the fairy god, Pan. I could hardly believe that anyone could make such a beautiful thing out of teeth! It was so inspiring. It made me want to start collecting teeth right away.

But I have to get through this course and pass my tooth fairy tests first...

I had lunch at the statue, then flew on to find the other three sites: the Enchanted Bridge,

Enamel Arch

and Snowdrop Palace, which sparkled as if it were bathed in dew. I could see why HR called them wonders.

I'd never seen anything as wonderful in my life.

I was the first one to arrive back at school, followed by Niamh and then, quite a lot later, by Mab. She'd dropped her map and couldn't find her way home!

Peasbody was feeling much better and she joined us. I showed everyone my pictures.

Peasbody whistled and said that she never knew Fairyland was so full of wonders.

We all laughed.

"And do you know the biggest wonder of all?" said HR.

"No," we said.

"The biggest wonder will be if you four make it through this course and become tooth fairies!" HR said, glaring at us.

If I ever see HR smile, that really will be a wonder!

Day
Seven

We spent today at the school's simulation centre learning the different ways of getting into human houses.

The centre is run by Skilly Widdens. He's quite old, like Hyacinth Rose, but he's much more smiley. He has twinkly blue eyes that always look as if they are laughing.

"Now, my little cherubs," he said, "I hope you're all enjoying your time at Tooth Fairy School and that they're treating you well."

"Yes, thank you," we all nodded.

He smiled. "That Hyacinth Rose can be a little thorny, but she's a dear petal at heart."

Peasbody grinned at me and I grinned back. HR is just about the last person we'd ever describe as a dear petal!

Skilly Widdens showed us round the simulation centre, which was set up like a human house. He gave us a plan of the house and asked us to mark all the means of entry. I found seven: windows, door, chimney, keyhole, letterbox, air vent and cat flap. Niamh and Peasbody found the same, but Mab did best of all – she found eight. Skilly Widdens congratulated her for finding the fairy's last resort: "When all else fails, use the mousehole!" he said.

Skilly Widdens told us that the best way for a tooth fairy to enter a human house is through a window – and best of all the window into the bedroom of the child whose tooth you have come to collect. He pulled down the window on the simulated house until it was only open by a few millimetres. He asked for a volunteer to try to get

through the tiny gap. We looked at
Skilly Widdens and at the window.
None of us fancied trying. You'd have
to be a mouse to do that, I thought.

Well, what happened next amazed
me. In less than a twinkling of an eye,
the little old fairy flapped his wings,
rose into the air and passed through
the gap beneath
the window.
An instant later
he was beaming
at us from
the other
side!

We could not believe our eyes!

"We fairies can get through the narrowest of gaps," said Skilly Widdens when he reappeared on our side of the glass.

"It's just a question of confidence."

After that, we all had a go. Skilly

Widdens was right, but it took us a
few attempts. On my first try I got
my wings trapped and was stuck
half in and half out of the room!
Skilly Widdens had to release me.

Niamh banged her nose on the
sill and Peasbody's wild hair got
tangled in the window latch.

Mab was the only one who managed
to pass through first time without a
hitch. It seems like she's getting the hang
of the course at last. She looked happy
for the first time since she got here.

Good old Mab!

Only one more week to go before
we take our test! Gulp!

Day
Eight

Today was our second day at the simulation centre. I much prefer these practical lessons with Skilly Widdens to those boring lectures by Madame le Fey. I wish it was all like this. HR overhead me saying this to Niamh this morning at breakfast and she wasn't pleased.

"Pip," she barked. "Tell me, what is the tooth fairies' motto?"

"The tooth, the whole tooth and nothing but the tooth, ma'am," I said.

"Precisely," huffed HR. "Not a little bit of the tooth, not the parts of the tooth that you fancy learning about. No, the whole tooth. Kindly remember that and I think you will come to thank Madame le Fey should you ever become a tooth fairy." She said it as if she thought this a very unlikely thing to happen.

I felt about half a centimetre tall, but I soon felt better once we got to the simulation centre. Skilly Widdens makes us work hard, but it's such fun. We did some more flying and passing-through-narrow-gaps practice today.

We started with windows again.

Then we moved on to the gaps
under doors,

keyholes

and letterboxes, and air vents.

We learnt how to pass through cat flaps without making any noise and to swoop down chimneys.

This was my favourite part — I love the rush of air as you whoosh down! Peasbody didn't like it at all though. She said chimneys made her feel "claustrophobic".

Skilly Widdens explained that claustrophobia is having a fear of small closed places. He said that he used to worry that he'd get trapped in the chimney and never get out. Niamh asked him how he had cured his fear and Skilly Widdens said that he went to see somebody who knew more than anyone else about going down chimneys.

"Who?" we asked.

"Why, Father Christmas, of course!" said Skilly Widdens, with a big smile.

He told us that Father Christmas

had said to him, "Look at me. See how big and round my tummy is? Well, there's never been a chimney yet that I couldn't get down — and if I can do it, why, a skinny fairy like you has nothing to worry about!"

Then Skilly Widdens looked at Peasbody and said, "I should say the same was true for you, wouldn't you?" His eyes were as blue and sparkly as dewy forget-me-nots and Peasbody looked happier at once.

When we'd finished our flying exercises, Skilly Widdens sat us down and told us to listen very carefully. His face was much more serious than usual.

"Now, my cherubs," he said. "It's not only clever wings that make a good tooth fairy. Getting into a human house can be a dangerous business. You need to keep your eyes open and your wits sharp.

Supposing, for instance, you are nudging your way silently through a cat flap at the very moment a great big tom cat is coming the other way. The outcome could be catastrophic!"

74

Then Skilly Widdens asked us
what we should always look out for
before we went down a chimney.

"Father Christmas?" asked Niamh
and we all laughed.

But Skilly Widdens looked serious.

He said we had to beware of smoke,
because we wouldn't want to go
tumbling down into a lighted fire
and burn our bottoms, would we?

We all shook our heads at that.

At the end of the lesson, Hyacinth Rose came in to see how we were getting on.

"Why, isn't this a pleasure," said Skilly Widdens, and his face lit up as if the sun had just come out.

"How are you today, my dear petal?" Yes, he really said it — to her face!

"Oh, er, fine, thank you, Mr Widdens," HR stammered and — guess what? — she blushed. She really did! Perhaps she does have feelings after all!

Day
Nine

We trainees were all a bit sleepy when we woke up today because last night we stayed awake till late asking each other riddles and telling stories.

Niamh told us about a cheeky boggart who was always playing tricks on people. Then Peasbody made up a funny riddle that made us all laugh:

"What's green and naughty and goes around kissing people?"

Answer: A snoggart!

This morning Madame le Fey gave us a lecture about how to recognize a good tooth and what coin we should leave in exchange. She showed us a chart and gave us a copy. More things to learn for our test next week! There is so much to remember. I was so tired that I couldn't keep my eyes open and I fell asleep in the middle of the lesson. Worse still, I started snoring! Niamh nudged me and I woke up with a yawn. For a moment, I didn't know where I was. Madame le Fey didn't look at all pleased. She said a tooth fairy must be awake and alert, not sleeping on the job.

"Sleeping is for children," she said.

I was worried that Madame le Fey might report me to Hyacinth Rose, but I don't think she did, because HR didn't say anything about it when she saw me later. In fact she seemed to be in quite a good mood.

"Fallen out of any beds lately, Pip?" she remarked, and I think she almost smiled!

Day
Ten

We were back with Skilly Widdens today. He told us we had to pay careful attention, because today's lesson was the most important of all. We had practised flying, we had learnt

how to enter houses and discovered
some of the hazards to look out for.
But now it was time to meet the
child.

We all let out a gasp at that,
because none of us had met a real
human child before.

But there wasn't a real child, it was just pretend. Skilly Widdens had made a child's bedroom in the centre. He said that when you enter the room, you first take a moment to be certain that the child is asleep. Next you swiftly and silently fly to the bed, positioning yourself by the pillow under which the tooth is waiting.

He paused there, standing by the bed and raising one finger.

"Now for the tricky part," he said. He showed us how to slide our hands very gently under the pillow

and remove the tooth. You have to
check whether there is a note under
the pillow. If there is, then you take
it out – very carefully – read it and
write a reply with the fairy pen and
paper which every tooth fairy carries.
When you have finished, you leave
the letter and the appropriate coin
under the pillow.

Then you fly away quickly using the nearest available exit.

Skilly Widdens said that at ordinary schools they teach the importance of the three Rs, but at tooth fairy school they teach the three Ss: speed, silence and stealth.

I asked him what stealth was and
he said it was being very quiet and
secret.

Then Mab put up her hand and
asked what would happen if you were
in the room and the child woke up.

Skilly Widdens smiled and said
that was a very good question,
but he wasn't going to answer it.
He was going to pass it over to
Hyacinth Rose.

We all looked round in surprise
because we didn't know HR was
there. She must have come into
the room very quietly when Skilly
Widdens was talking.

"I think you have a story to tell,
don't you?" said Skilly Widdens.

"I do," said HR. "Indeed I do."

Hyacinth Rose told us a story
about when she was a young tooth

fairy. She'd just passed her test and was on her very first solo mission. She found the right house and had no trouble getting in as the bedroom window was open. Everything was going fine when, suddenly, she realized the child was awake! It was a little girl and she was looking right at Hyacinth Rose. We looked at HR too, holding our breath, wondering what had happened next. Peasbody couldn't contain herself.

"What did you do?" she squealed.

"I panicked," HR confessed.

"I did what you should never do —

I returned the
child's stare."
She paused and
shook her head as if
telling herself off. Then she
went on to tell us that there are
three strict rules to follow when
dealing with a wakeful child:

    Rule I: Do not look the child
    in the eye.

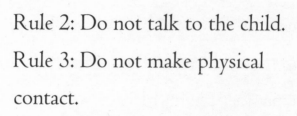

Rule 2: Do not talk to the child.

Rule 3: Do not make physical contact.

"Breaking these rules can be very dangerous," she said. "Humans and fairies simply do not mix. They have their world, we have ours."

"But what happened to you?" I asked.

HR gave me a stern gaze. She said that once the panic had passed, she started to think clearly again and remembered: if all else fails, use your fairy magic. So she uttered a spell of sleep and forgetfulness, which meant that when the child woke up the next day she wouldn't remember seeing HR.

For the rest of the lesson we practised removing the tooth from under the pillow, taking it in turns to be the child and the tooth fairy. It was much harder

than it looked when Skilly Widdens showed us. One time when I was being the tooth fairy, the tooth got stuck and I pulled so hard I flipped Peasbody right off the bed!

"Softly, Pip, softly," cooed Skilly Widdens.

By the end of the lesson, though, we were all pretty good at gentle tooth removal. Tomorrow's lesson is spells. I can't wait!

Day
Eleven

I had a letter from home this morning. The post fairies delivered it while I was asleep and when I woke up it was on the toadstool next to my hammock.

Dear Pip,

How are you, my blossom?
We miss you so much. Home isn't the
same without you — it's so quiet!
Your pa has been very busy designing
a new palace for the Fairy Queen.
It's going to be quite magnificent!
He's going to need lots of very good
teeth to make it, so you'd better pass your
test and get collecting! He's
asked me to choose the colours for
the flowers in the palace gardens,
so I shall be very busy too. A flower

fairy's work is never done, as they say! I hope you are getting along all right at school. I know Hyacinth Rose can appear rather stern at times, but underneath she has the kindest of hearts. Please send her my regards.

Big hugs,
Your loving Ma x

I was very excited, but when I'd read the letter, I started to cry. It made me realize how much I miss my family, even though I'm very happy here most of the time.

The others were very kind. Niamh told me about her home in the Emerald Isle, while Peasbody brought me breakfast in bed and Mab made me a beautiful daisy chain. After that, I felt much better. We've become such good friends. I hope we all pass and become tooth fairies together.

HR taught us spells today. She's an expert. Her spell books are in all the libraries. Even the Fairy Queen reads them!

The first thing HR taught us was the spell of sleep and forgetfulness. She said it was the most important spell and she made us all copy it out. It goes like this:

Close your eyes,
    my child, my sweet
Let sleep come swift
    on fairy feet
And when you rise
    not eye nor ear
Recall our brief encounter here.

It sounds simple enough, but a

spell is more than just the words
that you speak – it's how you say
them. The tone of your voice
must be just right.

"You must sound like you are
sleep itself," HR told us, and I
must admit that when she spoke
the spell, she really did. My eyelids
were drooping and Peasbody
actually fell asleep.

We had to get into pairs and
practise the spell on each other.
I paired up with Niamh. She was
brilliant. She has such a beautiful
lilting voice. I'd have been in my

bed and dozing in no time if we'd
been back in the dorm!

I found it much more difficult
when it was my turn. For a start I
kept getting the words wrong (and
you have to get every word exactly
right). I couldn't get the tone right
either. I sounded more like a
howling wind than sleep.

My wand control was terrible too. As you say the spell, you have to wave your wand in gentle circles, pointing it at your subject on the very last word. It's much harder than it sounds. Putting all those things together is a bit like trying to pat your head while rubbing your chest. (I can't do that either!) I'm going to have to do lots of spell practice before the tests, I can see!

I made up my own spell this evening:

Fairy spirits flying high,

Through the starry summer sky,

North and south, east and west,

Bring me luck to pass my test!

I hope it works!

Day
Twelve

Our lesson today was letter writing
and my hand is aching so much I can
hardly write this.

HR took us to the archive room
where all the letters ever written by
children to tooth fairies are stored.

There are boxes and
boxes of them –
millions and trillions
of letters from
children all over
the world. And,
of course, every
letter has to be
answered by the
tooth fairies!

"Children ask all
kinds of questions,"
said HR.
"You have to
be prepared for

anything – and have an answer
ready." She picked out a few
letters and read them to us.
They were full of questions.

Dear Tooth Fairy,
Please can
you tell
me how
tall you ar
Thank you
Sarah

Dear Too
Please
tell me
tooth
fall out

Dear Tooth Fairy,
Where do
you
all live?
How did
you know
my tooth
had fallen out?
Thank you,
Love Ella

What do you
want my tooth for?
From Zack

My head was spinning listening to them all! It must be very tiring being a human parent if children ask so many questions!

HR told us that there are three golden rules you must always remember when writing to a child (she likes her rules does HR!).

Rule 1: Be polite and friendly, but firm.

Rule 2: Always tell the truth.

Rule 3: Sign your letters from The Tooth Fairy – never reveal your real name.

This is most important. If you tell a mortal your real name, you will lose your fairy powers.

HR sat us down at desks in the archive room and gave us each a handful of old letters so we could practise writing answers. We each had an acorn cup of green ink and a fern frond to write with. My first letter was from Billy. He wanted £100 for his tooth! I was tempted to write: "Dear Billy, don't be so greedy." but I remembered the first golden rule, so instead I wrote this:

Dear Billy,
    Thank you for your letter. I am afraid
I cannot leave you £100. We tooth fairies have
fixed rates for teeth, depending on their condition.
    Please find the appropriate sum for your tooth
under your pillow.
    I look forward to doing business with you
again in the future.
                    Yours sincerely,
                    The Tooth Fairy

HR came by as I was finishing and
peered over my shoulder.

"Hmm, not bad, Pip," she said.

"You might just
make a tooth fairy yet."

"Thank you," I said smiling.
Actually, I was grinning from ear
to ear.

"Don't get carried away now,"
HR added. "It wasn't that good."
But she couldn't stop me smiling.

There was an interesting letter from
a girl called Tanzy, who wanted to
know what colour my wings were
and how fast I could fly. I thought
about making up a speed, but that

would have broken the second
golden rule, so I told the truth
and said that I didn't actually know,
but I'd always found I could fly
fast enough. I hoped that was a
good enough answer.

Of all the tasks we've been given
so far, I think this was the hardest.
You really had to use your brain —
and it was very tiring doing all that
writing. Peasbody says she's going
to have to wear her arm in a sling
tomorrow and I know what she
means.

Only two more days to go before the test. It gives me butterflies just thinking about it!

Day
Thirteen

Today was our last day in the
classroom (tomorrow we have a
study day to read through our notes
and practise our skills on our own).
We had a session with Madame le

Fey in the morning. Then after
lunch we went to the simulation
centre. We took it in turns to do
practice missions. Skilly Widdens
set little traps to test us. One time
I flew down the chimney (checking
first that there was no smoke)
and found it was blocked.
By the time
I'd turned
round and
flown back
out again, I was
all covered
in soot!

"Sorry, Pip," Skilly Widdens said. "People don't use their chimneys as much these days. Father Christmas finds it most inconvenient." I decided I would use the window in future!

Our last lesson was with Hyacinth Rose. She talked to us about what it meant to be a tooth fairy and what a responsible job it was. She also told us that when she was a trainee tooth fairy like us she'd had the best teacher – it was Skilly Widdens! So that's why he dared call her "dear petal", even though she is now a super expert teacher like him.

At the end of her lesson, she had a surprise for us. She said that because we had all worked so hard, she was going to give us a party that evening. Basil had prepared some delicious refreshments and the pixies had kindly offered to come and play their music for us.

Her usually stern face smiled. We
were all so amazed we couldn't speak.
And what a brilliant party it was!
Basil served up a feast. There were
honey and walnut cakes and saffron
cookies. There were trays of

scrumptious dogwood fruits that Basil calls pixie pears. We drank burdock nectar and the teachers drank nettle wine. Some will o' the wisps stopped by and lit up the party with their twinkling.

The pixies were great. When you hear the music of their pipes and

whistles, you just want to dance —
and dance we did in the moonlight.
HR danced with Skilly Widdens
and Madame le Fey danced with
Basil, and we danced with all the
pixies (even Mab — she wasn't
shy at all).

It was such fun! Niamh was
incredible! She has such quick
feet. And she has a beautiful
singing voice too. She sang a
couple of songs with the pixies
that were so sweet I swear there
were tears in Skilly Widdens's
eyes. It was truly magical.

We all agreed that it was the best night of our lives.

Day
Fourteen

The last day of our course!

I woke up quite late after last night's party and stayed in bed all morning reading through all those sheets that Madame le Fey gave us. There

is so much to remember.

It was a quietish day, but there
was excitement to come. Just
before dinner, HR summoned
the trainees to the lecture room.
When we arrived Skilly Widdens
and Madame le Fey were there too.
They each said a few words to

wish us luck in tomorrow's test
and told us to stay calm.

We thought that was it but
then HR lifted four beautiful
bags from under her desk and
put them on the table. Each kit
bag contained all the things we
might need when we go out on
our first missions tomorrow night.
HR said that no tooth fairy could
go about her business without the
right equipment – and neither
should we.

She fixed us with one of her steely
stares. "If you succeed,

these will be yours to keep for ever,"
she said.

She called us up one by one to
receive them. It was such a thrilling
moment. The tips of my wings
tingled when I stepped forward to
collect my bag – and what a gorgeous
bag it is! It's got different coloured
stripes, like a rainbow, and a pink

handle. I couldn't wait to
get back to the dorm
to look at it more closely.
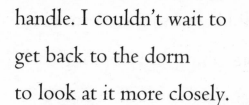

Inside each bag is a wand,
tooth fairy ID,
writing paper,
envelopes,
a pen (glittery, of course!), a map,
fairy dust, a tooth collection box, a
wallet of different coins and a tiny
spell book for emergencies.

We danced around the dorm with our bags laughing and shouting and feeling like proper tooth fairies — until HR popped her head round the door and told us it was time for bed.

"We don't want any sleepyheads tomorrow," she said — and I think she was looking at ME!

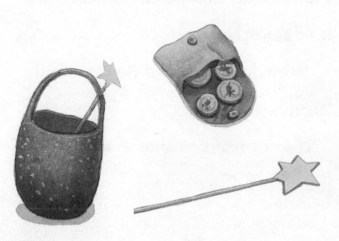

When HR left it all went very quiet. I suppose we were getting nervous about tomorrow – I know I was. Mab looked through her spell book and said she wished there was a spell to stop nerves. Peasbody said that she wished there was a spell that would make us all pass the test tomorrow. I remembered the spell I'd made up the other night and told it to the others.

"Why don't we try it now?" asked Niamh.

"It's not really magic," I said. "It's just a spell I made up."

"Isn't all magic made up by someone?" said Niamh.

So we held hands and formed a fairy ring, then closed our eyes and recited my good luck spell.

"Fairy spirits flying high,
Through the starry summer sky,
North and south, east and west,
Bring us luck to pass our test!"

Day
Fifteen

The exams begin!

I got woken up by the bluebell alarm to find the post fairies had delivered another letter from home. It was a good luck card from Ma and Pa.

At breakfast there was my favourite hazelnut crunch but I was much too nervous to eat.

After breakfast HR took us to the school examination room where Madame le Fey was waiting to hand out our test papers.

"Bonne chance, mes filles," she said, and she looked at the clock. "Alons-y! Begin!"

When I first looked at the paper, I panicked. The questions seemed to float around on the page and I couldn't get my mind to focus. Then I remembered about staying calm. I closed my eyes and took some deep breaths. The paper wasn't really that difficult. I could answer most of the questions OK.

After the exam, we had the rest of the day off to relax until the evening. And if we'd been nervous about the written exam, that was nothing compared with the mission we'd be flying tonight. You couldn't predict what would happen.

We tried to distract ourselves by playing a game of hide and seek.

The others found me easily, but when it was my turn to seek I couldn't find them at all. I hoped that wasn't a bad omen for my mission.

Each of us was to be accompanied on our mission by a qualified tooth fairy, who would act as our examiner and our minder in case anything went wrong. When the time came for us to begin, Skilly Widdens came to fetch us.

"Well, my cherubs, here's the moment you've been waiting for," he said with his twinkly smile. He handed each of us an envelope.

With trembling fingers I ripped mine open ... and gasped. I was to collect the tooth of a boy named Nathaniel.

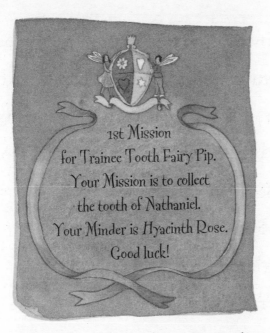

1st Mission
for Trainee Tooth Fairy Pip.
Your Mission is to collect
the tooth of Nathaniel.
Your Minder is Hyacinth Rose.
Good luck!

But it was the other name that made me gasp. My minder was Hyacinth Rose!

"I am merely an observer, Pip," HR said to me as I waited to set off on my mission. "Just try to forget that I am here."

How was I supposed to forget that my tutor would be watching every move I made – and probably tutting and giving me her withering look too! I felt like giving up there and then – but I didn't. I wanted to be a tooth fairy more than anything and I was determined to do my best.

I'll just have to prove to HR that I've got what it takes, I said to myself. Then Skilly Widdens chimed the bluebell gong and it was time to fly. As I rose into the air, I heard a soft voice calling, "Good luck, Pip. Make your mother proud." Was it HR –

or did I imagine it? I'm still not
sure, but it gave me a real lift.

It was a lovely night for flying. I
checked my map a couple of times,
but I had no trouble finding my way.

As I got closer to Nathaniel's house,
I felt the tips of my wings tingle.
That meant the tooth was there
waiting for me. So far, so good!

I reached the house and quickly
managed to find Nathaniel's room.
I peeped in at the window to make
sure the boy was asleep, which he was.
But now I faced my first test: how was
I to get in? The window was shut fast
– there wasn't even a gap that a fairy
could squeeze through. The chimney
was blocked up, so I was just thinking
about gathering my courage to try an
air vent in the wall (I don't like air

vents – they smell funny and you
don't know what's going to be on
the other side) when there was a
clatter below me.

A big ginger cat appeared and
swaggered out into the garden.
That made my mind up: I'd enter
through the cat flap!

In moments I was down at the back door and through the cat flap without a sound – Skilly Widdens would have been proud of me.

It was the first time I'd ever been in a human house and the first thing that struck me was the smell – or smells. There were lots of them and they were a bit strong for my fairy nose. It reminded me of a boggart I met once. He was smelly too!

Inside the house it was very dark and very quiet, but I found Nathaniel's bedroom without any problem. The door was open and I flew in.

Nathaniel was fast asleep and snoring. I flew over to his bed and put my hand under the pillow. The tooth was there all right – and there was a note too. I pushed the pillow up a bit and wiggled the tooth this way and that till it came out. I examined it first to make sure it wasn't a forgery, then I checked to see what condition it was in. The colour was fine, but it had some marks on it and the top was chipped. It wasn't good enough for a gold coin, nor bad enough for a bronze one. I took a silver coin out of my wallet and left it under the pillow.

Now I read the note:

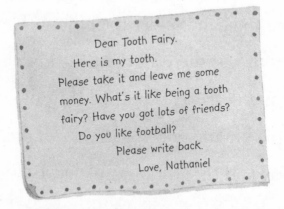

Dear Tooth Fairy,
Here is my tooth.
Please take it and leave me some
money. What's it like being a tooth
fairy? Have you got lots of friends?
Do you like football?
Please write back.
Love, Nathaniel

I sat down at the end of the bed,
took out my pen and started to write
a reply. I thanked Nathaniel for his
letter and told him that I couldn't
really answer his question about
what it was like to be a tooth fairy
because I was only a trainee and

this was my very first mission. I said I was enjoying myself very much so far, though, and I thought that being a tooth fairy was probably the best job in the world. I told him that I had some very good friends who were also trainee tooth fairies like me (but I remembered not to say their names!).

I was just considering how to answer his question about football when I glanced up and got an enormous shock – Nathaniel's eyes were open and he was staring right at me!

For an instant I froze. My mind went blank. I couldn't do anything.

"Who a—a—are you?" Nathaniel stammered.

"I'm ... the Tooth Fairy," I muttered, just stopping myself in time from revealing my name. I gazed around the room in a blind panic, trying to get my mind to think, when suddenly my eyes caught sight of HR hovering just outside the window. Seeing her made my brain start to work. This was exactly what had happened to her on her first mission, wasn't it? I would just have to do what she had done.

Quickly I took my wand from
my bag and waved it in circles as
I uttered the spell of sleep and
forgetfulness. I said it perfectly,

even pointing my wand on the last
word. Nathaniel's eyes drooped and
his head fell back on the pillow.
A moment later he was snoring.
I sighed with relief. Then I finished

my letter and tucked it under the pillow. The window was shut but not locked and I managed to lift it just enough to squash myself through.

Once outside, I flew like the wind for home. I was so tired after the excitement of the mission that I fell asleep as soon as I got into my hammock. I dreamt about teeth – talking teeth! But they kept telling me that I would never be a tooth fairy…

Day Sixteen

Our last day!

When I finally woke up, I heard the others whispering. They were discussing their missions, so I got up and joined them. They all wanted to know about my mission and how it had been having HR as my minder. So I told them everything that had happened. They gasped when I told them about the boy waking up. They'd had much more straightforward missions than mine. The biggest drama was when Peasbody left her bag behind in the room and had to go back for it.

We'd done the tests, now we had to wait for the results. It took all morning for our teachers to decide if we were good enough to become

tooth fairies. It was the longest
morning of our lives!

After lunch they were finally ready.
We were summoned to HR's office
one by one.

First to go was Mab.

She was so nervous her wings were
quivering! A little while later she came
back ... smiling.

"I passed," she said shyly and her

face went bright pink.

"Well done, Mab!" we shouted and we all gave her a hug.

Next it was Niamh's turn.

She came back with a smile too. Then Peasbody was called. She was gone longer than the other two and she came out of HR's office looking gloomy as a gnome. We were just getting ready to comfort her, when her face broke into a gigantic grin.

"Fooled you," she cried. "I passed!"
It was just another one of her tricks.

Now it was my turn. Niamh
said they were saving the best for
last, but I'd been playing over the
events of yesterday in my head
and I was sure I was going to fail.
Not only had HR seen me making

eye contact with a child, but she'd seen me talking to him too. Then there was the written test – what if I'd got the spells all wrong?

As I opened the door to HR's office, I knew my dream was over. I wasn't going to be a tooth fairy after all. A tear trickled down my cheek.

"Why Pip, whatever's the matter?" said HR brusquely. "We haven't said anything yet."

"Cheer up, my cherub," said Skilly Widdens, and looking into his kind eyes made me feel better.

Madame le Fey handed me my written test results — and they were excellent!

"Well, it seems you didn't sleep through all my lessons, Pip," she said.

Now it was time for the results of my mission — but I still didn't think I'd pass.

Skilly Widdens smiled. He began by saying that I was very lucky to have had Hyacinth Rose as my observer. (Lucky, I thought. You must be joking!)

He said that HR had told him

about my difficulties (here we go, I thought) and how excellently I had dealt with them. I couldn't believe it. Had I heard right? Then Skilly Widdens said that I had proved myself a most resourceful and intelligent fairy and that my mission had been an outstanding success.

"Well done, my cherub," said Skilly Widdens.

I was so amazed, I didn't know what to say.

"So, Pip, you have passed both your written and practical tests with

flying colours," HR declared –
and now even she was smiling! "I am
delighted to tell you that you are
now officially a Tooth Fairy,
First Class. Congratulations!"
And she handed me my pass note.

It's really true! I passed! I'm a
Tooth Fairy! This is the best,
most wonderful day of my life.
I think I must be the happiest
fairy alive!

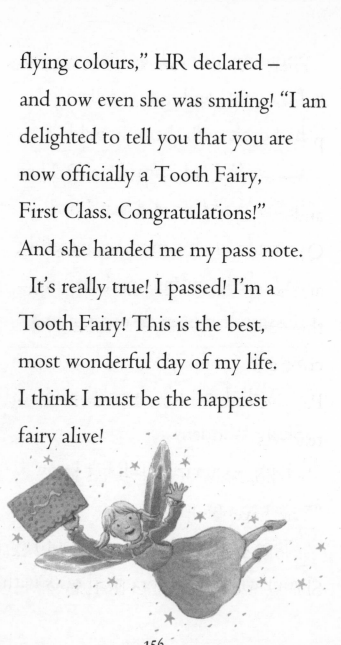

There was just time to tell the others before we rushed off to the presentation ceremony.

We were given our pass certificates and coloured wing tips by the Fairy Queen herself! My wing tips are pink and so are Niamh's. Ma and Pa were there and they looked so proud. Ma cried and I think there was a tear in Pa's eye too! I introduced them to my teachers.

"Hello, May," HR greeted Ma. "You haven't changed a bit."

"Nor have you, Hyacinth," said Ma. She went on to explain that she and

Hyacinth Rose were at school together, and that the stories she told me about tooth fairies when I was a baby were about HR! So really HR is responsible for me being a tooth fairy!

Most thrilling of all was meeting the Fairy Queen. She is so beautiful – and very excited about the new palace Pa is building for her.

"You'll have to get us some tip top teeth, Pip," Pa said and I told him that I'd get right on to it.

Tonight I'm off to visit a girl called Anna. Her tooth has fallen out and I just know that it's going to be a very good one! Put that tooth under your pillow, Anna, here comes the Tooth Fairy!

Yup, that's me, Pip, Tooth Fairy – FIRST CLASS!

Her Royal Majesty,

the Fairy Queen, is delighted to confirm that

Pip

has passed her Tooth Fairy Examinations

and is now a Tooth Fairy (First Class).

Congratulations!

The Fairy Queen